Feeling WORRIED!

Published in North America by Free Spirit Publishing Inc., Minneapolis, Minnesota, 2017

Library of Congress Cataloging-in-Publication Data
Names: Barnham, Kay, author. | Gordon, Mike, 1948 March 16– illustrator.
Title: Feeling worried! / written by Kay Barnham ; illustrated by Mike Gordon.
Description: Minneapolis, Minnesota : Free Spirit Publishing Inc., 2017. | Series: Everyday Feelings
Identifiers: LCCN 2017008395| ISBN 9781631982552 (hardcover) | ISBN 1631982559 (hardcover)
Subjects: LCSH: Worry in children—Juvenile literature. | Worry—Juvenile literature.
Classification: LCC BF723.W67 W66 2017 | DDC 155.4/1246—dc23 LC record available at https://lccn.loc.gov/2017008395

Free Spirit Publishing does not have control over or assume responsibility for author or third-party websites and their content.

Reading Level Grade 2; Interest Level Ages 5–9; Fountas & Pinnell Guided Reading Level M

10 9 8 7 6 5 4 3 2 1
Printed in China
H13660517

Free Spirit Publishing Inc.
6325 Sandburg Road, Suite 100
Minneapolis, MN 55427-3674
(612) 338-2068
help4kids@freespirit.com
www.freespirit.com

First published in 2017 by Wayland, a division of Hachette Children's Books · London, UK, and Sydney, Australia
Text © Wayland 2017
Illustrations © Mike Gordon 2017

The rights of Kay Barnham to be identified as the author and Mike Gordon as the illustrator of this Work have been asserted in accordance with the Copyright, Designs and Patents Act, 1988.

Managing editor: Victoria Brooker
Creative design: Paul Cherrill

feeling
WORRIED!

Written by
Kay Barnham

Illustrated by
Mike Gordon

free spirit
PUBLISHING®

School was over for the day
and the long, warm afternoon
lay ahead. "As soon as I get home,
I'm going to play on my scooter,"
Ava said.

"Lucky you," said her
brother, Noah. "I have to
do my math homework."

"Oh, that won't take you long," said Ava.
She couldn't believe it when a tear
rolled down Noah's cheek.

"What's wrong?" asked Ava. She hated it
when her brother was upset.
"The homework looks really, really hard,"
sobbed Noah. "I keep looking at it and I don't
know what I'm supposed to do. I'm so worried
that Mr. Skinner will be mad at me."

"Try not to worry, Noah," said Ava. "We'll look at the homework together. It might not be as tricky as you think."

Ten minutes later, they sat in the kitchen.
"Let's check out the first question," said Ava.
"Look, all you have to do is add those
numbers and then multiply them by 5."
"That's all?" asked Noah.

"That's all," said Ava.

"And I've spent all week worrying about it,"
said Noah, rolling his eyes.
"Next time, I'll just give it a try!"

At school the next day, Ava heard some very sad news. Bahar's parents were splitting up. "Are you okay?" Ava asked Bahar.

"Not really," said Bahar. "I love my mom
and dad. Now I don't know which one I'm going
to live with. And I'm just so worried that I
won't get to see them both."

Ava frowned. She didn't know what would happen either. "Have you asked your mom and dad about it?" she said.

Bahar shook her head.
"Try it," said Ava. "They both love you.
They might be able to help you feel
better with some answers."

The next day,
Bahar looked a little happier.
"Did you ask your parents
about the divorce?" said Ava.

Bahar nodded. "They told me that
I'll live with my mom, but I'll stay with my dad
every Wednesday and every other weekend.
I'll see him during school breaks, too.
I'm so glad I talked to them."

The next week, Mrs. Russo had a surprise
for the class—a brand-new student!
"Let me introduce you to Mila,"
said the teacher. "She moved
here from Australia. Please
help her feel welcome."

Ava smiled at the new girl,
but Mila barely looked up.

Even though everyone tried to talk to Mila, the new girl just shrugged and wouldn't speak. Soon, most of them stopped trying. But Ava was determined to help.

"What's wrong?" she asked Mila. "Nothing," mumbled the new girl. She twisted a braid around her finger. "Really?" said Ava. "I'm worried everyone will laugh at me when I talk," Mila whispered at last.

"What's wrong with the way you talk?"
asked Ava, puzzled.
"Well, nothing," said Mila. "But I come
from Australia. So that means I talk
differently than everyone else at this school.
They'll think I sound funny."

"So that's why you've been so quiet!" Ava said. "Well, I think you sound great.

Now come and meet my friends. And don't worry. They'll love your accent, too, I promise."

That evening, it was Ava's turn to feel worried.
Tomorrow, she and Noah were going to
the dentist. And she was not
looking forward to it *at all*.

What if the dentist wanted to poke
at her teeth? What if she got in trouble
for not brushing enough? What if
she needed a filling?

The next morning, Ava was still worried.

"What's wrong?" asked Mom at breakfast time. "Why aren't you eating? Don't you feel well?"

Ava stared at her cereal. "I'm worried about going to the dentist," she admitted glumly. "My stomach is churning so much that I don't feel even a little bit hungry."

"Come on, eat up. The dentist is there
to help care for your teeth, not to shout at you,"
said Mom. "You can brush your teeth before
we go. But first, I have an idea …"

After breakfast, Mom pretended to be
the dentist, while Ava was the patient.
It was lots of fun. Soon they were laughing
so much that Noah joined in, too.
And then so did Dad.

Later that morning, the real dentist didn't seem so scary. When Ava sat in the dentist's chair, she pictured her mom pretending to be a dentist, and that made her forget her worry.

"What a great patient you are," the dentist said.
"I *was* a bit worried," Ava admitted.
"But then I remembered something
really funny and I felt a lot better."
"Excellent," said the dentist. "It's *so* much easier
to check someone's teeth when they're smiling!"

NOTES FOR PARENTS AND TEACHERS

The aim of this book is to help children think about their feelings in an enjoyable, interactive way. Encourage kids to have fun pointing out details in the illustrations, making sound effects, and role playing. Here are more ideas for getting the most out of the book:

★ Encourage children to talk about their own feelings, if they feel comfortable doing so, either while you are reading the book or afterward. Here are some conversation prompts to try:

  · When are some times you feel worried? Why?

  · How do you stop feeling worried at those times?

  · Sometimes we might worry about things we can't change. Other worries may be about situations we *can* change or get help with. How could it help to know which kind of worry we're feeling?

  · This story talks about lots of things that people may feel worried about, such as difficult homework or a trip to the dentist. What other things might worry people?

★ Have children make face masks showing worried expressions. Ask them to explain how these faces show worry.

★ Put on a feelings play! Ask groups of children to act out the different scenarios in the book. The children could use their face masks to show when they are worried in the play.

★ Have kids make colorful word clouds. They can start by writing the word *worried,* then add any related words they think of, such as *anxious* or *nervous.* Have children write their words using different colored pens, making the most important words the biggest and less important words smaller.

★ Invite children to talk about the physical sensations that being worried can bring and where in their bodies they feel worry. Then discuss things we can do when we feel worried, such as talk to someone who cares about us, exercise, or focus on positive and reassuring thoughts.

★ A frown can show that someone is worried. A smile can show that someone is happy. Scientists aren't sure whether frowning or smiling uses more muscles. Have kids try frowning and then smiling and ask what *they* think the answer is. How do they feel when making each expression?

★ Ask kids to draw pictures of themselves feeling worried, using pencils to add frown lines. Then have them erase their frowns and imagine their worries disappearing.

For even more ideas to use with this series, download the free Everyday Feelings Leader's Guide at www.freespirit.com/leader.

Note: If a child continually worries or acts out often due to worry or anxiety, seek help from a counselor, psychologist, or other health specialist.

BOOKS TO SHARE

A Book of Feelings by Amanda McCardie, illustrated by Salvatore Rubbino
(Walker, 2016)

But What If? by Sue Graves, illustrated by Desideria Guicciardini
(Free Spirit Publishing, 2015)

F Is for Feelings by Goldie Millar and Lisa A. Berger, illustrated by
Hazel Mitchell (Free Spirit Publishing, 2014)

The Great Big Book of Feelings by Mary Hoffman, illustrated by Ros Asquith
(Frances Lincoln, 2016)

When I Feel Worried by Cornelia Maude Spelman, illustrated by
Kathy Parkinson (Albert Whitman & Company, 2013)

Wilma Jean the Worry Machine by Julia Cook, illustrated by
Anita DuFalla (National Center for Youth Issues, 2012)